Nemo was a little clownfish who lived on the Great Barrier Reef with his dad.

He was eager to start school and learn about the wonders of the ocean.

Little did Nemo know that both he and his dad were about to embark

on an amazing adventure. If you want to hear the story, you can read along

with me in your book. You'll know it is time to turn the page

when you hear this sound....

Let's begin now.

Narrator:	Matt Frewer
Marlin:	Albert Brooks
Coral:	Elizabeth Perkins
Nemo:	Alexander Gould
Dory:	Ellen DeGeneres
Bruce:	Barry Humphries
Chum:	Bruce Spence
Anchor:	Eric Bana
Dentist:	Bill Hunter
Bloat:	Brad Garrett
Gill:	Willem Dafoe
Deb (& Flo):	Vicki Lewis
Gurgle:	Austin Pendleton
Peach:	Allison Janney
Bubbles:	Stephen Root
Jacques:	Joe Ranft
Moonfish:	John Ratzenberger
Crush:	Andrew Stanton
Squirt:	Nick Bird
Nigel:	Geoffrey Rush

Read-along Executive Producer Ted Kryczko
Read-along story produced by Randy Thornton
Engineer/Associate Producer Jeff Sheridan

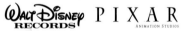

℗ 2014 Walt Disney Records/Pixar Animation Studios
© 2015 Disney/Pixar. All rights reserved.

This edition published by Parragon Books Ltd in 2015

Parragon Books Ltd
Chartist House
15–17 Trim Street
Bath BA1 1HA, UK
www.parragon.com

Copyright © 2015 Disney Enterprises, Inc. and Pixar

ISBN 978-1-4748-0547-6

Printed in China

Bath • New York • Cologne • Melbourne • Delhi
Hong Kong • Shenzhen • Singapore • Amsterdam

Deep in the ocean off the coast of Australia, a clownfish named Marlin showed his wife, Coral, their new home – a cosy anemone perched on a steep cliff called the Drop-off.

"So, you do like it, don't you?"

"Shhh! You're gonna wake the kids." Coral gazed at a nearby grotto that was filled with hundreds of fish eggs. "We still have to name them. I like Nemo." The happy couple played and teased each other, sharing their dreams of parenthood. As Marlin watched, Coral swam outside, straight into the view of a hungry barracuda!

Coral, worried about the eggs, edged toward the grotto. Marlin tried to stop her. "Coral, don't. They'll be fine. Just get inside. You. Right now!"

Coral broke for the grotto. The barracuda attacked. Marlin tried to block the hungry fish but was knocked against the cliff and everything went black. When he came to, there was only silence. "Coral! Coral?" The grotto was empty, and Coral was gone. "No."

Then he saw it – a single egg, slightly damaged.
Marlin cradled the egg in his fin. "I promise, I will
never let anything happen to you ... Nemo."

As time passed, Nemo grew into a happy young fish that was curious about everything. "How old are sea turtles?"

His father smiled. "Well, you know what? If I ever meet a sea turtle, I'll ask him."

Nemo longed for adventure, but Marlin, determined to protect him, barely let Nemo out of his sight.

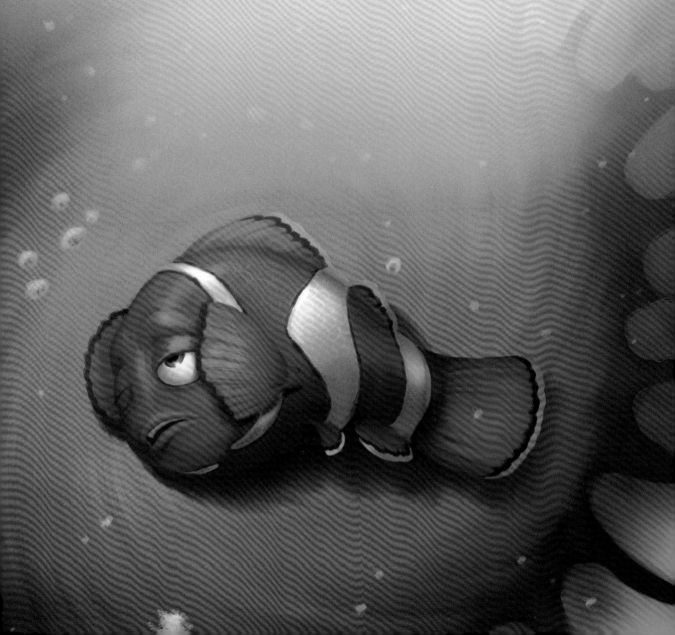

On Nemo's first day at school, Marlin panicked when he learned the class was going on a field trip to the Drop-off. Swimming after them, he heard Nemo and his new friends daring each other to swim out over the edge. Marlin called out to his son. "Nemo, you know you can't swim well."

"I can swim fine, Dad. Okay?"

"No, it's not okay! You know what? We'll start school in a year or two."

Nemo glared at him. "I hate you."

In defiance, Nemo darted up toward a boat on the surface. His father yelled after him. "Get back here! I said, get back here, now!"

As Nemo swam, a diver appeared behind him. Nemo screamed. "Ah! Daddy! Help me!"

Marlin tried to help but was blinded by a bright flash. It was a second diver, taking pictures. The first diver pulled out a net bag and caught Nemo. Then the two divers returned to the boat and sped off, accidentally knocking one of their masks overboard. Marlin shouted as he chased after the boat.

"Nemo! Nemo, no! NO!"

Marlin searched frantically. "Has anybody seen a boat? Please?" He bumped into a blue tang named Dory who offered to help.

"Hey, I've seen a boat! It went this way! Follow me!" When Marlin followed, Dory whirled around.

"Stop following me, okay?"

"What are you talking about? You're showing me which way the boat went."

Dory shook her head sadly. "I'm so sorry. See, I – I suffer from short-term memory loss."

Figuring Dory would be of no help, Marlin turned to leave and found himself face to face with a shark!

The shark bared his razor-like teeth and invited the two fish to a get-together with his friends. Marlin tried to decline, but Dory wouldn't hear of it.

"You mean like a party?"

"Yeah, right. A party. What do you say?"

The shark took them to a sunken ship surrounded by floating sea mines. Inside were two other sharks, and together they recited a pledge. "I am a nice shark, not a mindless eating machine. Fish are friends, not food." As they spoke, Marlin glanced up and saw a familiar object.

It was the diver's mask! Marlin told the sharks what had happened to Nemo. The first shark, whose name was Bruce, couldn't help but feel sorry. "Now, there is a father. Lookin' for his little boy...."

While Bruce sniffled, Marlin noticed writing on the mask. Could this be a clue to finding Nemo? Dory got excited. "Well then, we gotta find a fish that can read this!" She grabbed the mask, but bumped her nose, and Bruce got a whiff of blood.

"Oh, that's good! I'm having fish tonight!" As his friends tried to stop him, Bruce chased Marlin and Dory through the ship. They escaped with the mask by lodging a torpedo in Bruce's mouth. Unfortunately he spit out the torpedo, and it hit the surrounding sea mines. There was a huge explosion!

Miles away, Nemo found himself in a fish tank at a dentist's office with a goofy gang of tropical fish. All of them had come from pet stores except for their leader, Gill. Like Nemo, Gill had grown up in the ocean and he had a damaged fin from his attempts to escape the tank. The gang and their friend Nigel, a pelican, amused themselves by watching the dentist work.

Approaching the tank, the dentist showed Nemo a photo of Darla, his seven-year-old niece. "She's gonna be here Friday to pick you up. You're her present!" The fish gasped. Darla was a fish killer!

That night, Nemo's new friends held a ceremony at the tank's bubbling volcano, led by Bloat, the blowfish.

"Nemo, you have been called forth to the summit of Mount Wannahockaloogie to join with us in the fraternal bonds of tankhood ... if you are able to swim through ... the Ring of Fire!"

A ring of bubbles shot out, and Nemo swam through! Cheering, the fish named him Sharkbait. Gill swam forward. "Okay, Sharkbait's one of us now, agreed? We're gonna get him outta here. We're gonna help him escape," Gill explained.

If they could jam the filter, the dentist would have to clean the tank. When he put the fish in plastic bags, they could escape by rolling out the window and into the harbour!

The next day, Gill saw the dentist leave the room.

"That's your cue, Sharkbait!" Swimming to the surface, Nemo leaped into the filter and wedged a pebble between the gears. The fan stopped, shutting down the filter. "I got it! I got it!"

But as Nemo swam to escape, the pebble came loose, and the filter started up again, sucking Nemo toward the fan blades.

"Help me!"

Gill yanked a plant from the tank floor and fed it into the filter. "Sharkbait, grab hold of this!"

Nemo grabbed the tip of it, and the gang pulled him to safety. Gill knew he could never risk Nemo's life again.

"No. We're done."

Beneath the ocean, Marlin and Dory had survived the submarine explosion, but the diver's mask had fallen into a deep crevice. Swimming into the darkness, they saw a light. It was a lure on the antenna of a vicious anglerfish.

As the hungry fish closed in, it lit up the sea floor.
There was the mask. Suddenly Dory remembered she
could read human! Marlin courageously held the light
while she read. "P. Sherman, 42 Wallaby Way, Sydney."

Then Marlin cried out. "Duck!"

The anglerfish crashed above them, wedging himself
between the mask and a rock. Marlin breathed a sigh of
relief. They were still alive!

Escaping the crevice, Marlin and Dory spotted a school
of moonfish. The moonfish liked Dory and entertained her
with impressions of a lobster, a clipper ship, even Marlin.
When asked, her new friends provided directions to Sydney.

"What you want to do is follow the EAC. That's the East
Australian Current ... that direction."

Marlin and Dory headed for the EAC, but in their path was a
forest of deadly jellyfish. Marlin made it through, but a jellyfish stung
Dory and trapped her in its tentacles. Marlin pulled her out, but the
stings had made him weak and tired. The last thing he saw was the
silhouette of a giant sea turtle. When Marlin came to, he was lying on
the sea turtle's shell. The turtle spoke.

"Duuude! Name's Crush."

"Okay Crush. Listen, I need to get to the East Australian Current. EAC?"

"You're ridin' it, dude!" Around them, hundreds of sea turtles rode a ribbon of blue. One of them, Crush's son Squirt, was playing with Dory. When they finished playing, Marlin told Squirt the story of his search for Nemo.

"I live on this reef a long, long way from here...."

Squirt told the story to a lobster, the lobster told a dolphin and soon the news spread all the way to Sydney, where Nigel the pelican heard it.

Nigel sped to the dentist's office to tell Nemo.

"Your dad's been fightin' the entire ocean looking for you. And the word is, he's headed this way right now – to Sydney!"

"My father? Marlin?"

Nigel nodded. "That's it! Marlin! The little clownfish from the reef!"

"Really?" Inspired, Nemo grabbed a pebble and leaped into the filter again. This time, the pebble stuck, stopping the filter.

Gill and the others cheered. "Sharkbait! You did it!" Now the tank fish had to get the tank dirty so the dentist would have to clean it.

Outside Sydney, Marlin
and Dory said goodbye to the sea
turtles and left the EAC. Despite Marlin's best efforts to stop her, Dory
asked a whale for directions – in whale talk. As the whale swam closer,
hundreds of screaming shrimp raced past.

"Swim away!" But it was too late. Marlin and Dory were swept
into the whale's mouth.

Marlin was upset. He had come too far to end his trip like this!
Dory, meanwhile, remained optimistic. As the whale raised his tongue,
she asked him what was going on.

"He says it's time to let go. Everything's gonna be all right."

Marlin gulped and let go. They shot down the whale's throat and
up the spout, high into the air! Before them lay the skyline of Sydney.

In the dentist's office, the tank fish woke up Friday morning to a shocking sight. The tank was clean! The filter had been changed during the night, ruining their escape plan. To make matters worse, the dentist slipped a net into the water, capturing Nemo.

"Help me!"

Gill, thinking fast, charged into the net and shouted to Nemo. "Swim down!" He did, pulling down the net, and they escaped. But as Nemo fled, he swam straight into a plastic bag the dentist was holding. As the dentist lifted him out, the office door slammed open with a crash. Darla had arrived.

In Sydney Harbour, Marlin searched for the boat that took Nemo. "Come on, Dory, we're gonna find it." Suddenly, a pelican dove from the sky and scooped them up in its beak. It landed on a pier and tried to swallow them. Marlin wedged himself in its throat.

"No! I didn't come this far to be breakfast!" The pelican coughed. His friend Nigel came to help him and out flopped the fish. Marlin gasped.

"I gotta find my son, Nemo!"

Nigel grinned. "Hey, I know where your son is ... huh?!"
But he wasn't the only one watching. A flock of hungry seagulls swooped
down on Marlin and Dory. Nigel rescued them and sped off toward the city.
"Everybody, hold on!"

The dentist, meanwhile, greeted Darla. But when he reached for the plastic bag, he saw Nemo inside, apparently dead. Nemo winked and the gang cheered. "He's gonna get flushed down the toilet. He's gonna get outta here!"

But the dentist headed to the trashcan instead. "Oh no, not the trashcan! Nemo, no!" There was a crash and Nigel came hurtling through the window with Marlin and Dory in his beak. Surprised, the dentist dropped the bag, and it sprang a leak. Marlin peered out of Nigel's beak. He saw Nemo floating upside down in the bag.

"Nemo!"

"Gotcha!" The dentist grabbed Nigel's throat and closed his beak, trapping Marlin and Dory inside. Then he hurled Nigel out the window. "Out with ya! And stay out!"

Nemo looked up. "Daddy? Daddy?!" But it was too late. His father was gone. Just then, Darla reached for the bag and shook it. Gill called to the others. "Quick! To the top of Mount Wannahockaloogie!"

The gang tilted the volcano, and Gill swam inside.

"Ring of Fire!" Jaques the cleaner shrimp turned on the air bubbles, and Gill shot from the tank, landing on Darla's head! She screamed, dropping Nemo onto a dental mirror. Gill dove onto the other end, flipping Nemo into the sink and down the drain.

"Tell your dad I said hi!"

Nigel, shut out of the office, returned to the harbour. He dropped Marlin and Dory into the water. "I'm ... I'm so sorry. Truly I am."

Nigel flew off, and Marlin swam out to sea, leaving Dory. "I'm going home now."

As Marlin left, Nemo emerged from a nearby pipe. He spotted Dory swimming in circles. "Are you all right?"

"I think I lost somebody, but I ... I can't remember."

"I'm Nemo." He told her he was looking for someone too. They could look together. It wasn't until Dory saw the word "Sydney" on a pipe that she remembered who he was. Her eyes opened wide. "Ahh! You're Nemo!"

"You know my father? Where is he?"

"This way! He went this way! Quick!" They searched for Marlin, finding him in the nearby fishing grounds. A big net was dropped into the water. "Look out!" Marlin and Nemo escaped the net, but Dory wasn't so lucky.

"Help! Help!" Nemo thought of the net at the dentist's office. "We have to tell all the fish to swim down together. I can do this!"

Marlin tried to stop him. "No! I am not going to lose you again." But, watching Nemo, Marlin saw that his son had changed. And so had he. "You're right. I know you can."

Nemo grinned at his father. "Lucky fin!"

"Now, go! Hurry!"

As the net rose, Nemo swam up inside. "We have to tell everybody to – "

" – swim down together! Swim down!" It was Marlin, just outside, helping spread the word.

The fish swam down. Little by little, the net stopped rising and began to move down. Finally it broke off from the boat and unravelled. Dory and the others were free! But one fish was missing. On the ocean floor, Nemo lay trapped beneath the net. Marlin and Dory raced over and lifted the net, but Nemo didn't move. Marlin gasped.

"Nemo! Nemo?" The little clownfish lay motionless.

Then, after a moment, he coughed. "Daddy?"

Marlin sighed. "Oh, thank goodness."

"Dad. I don't hate you."

"Oh, no, no, no. I'm so sorry, Nemo."

Nemo reached out and touched his father's fin.

Marlin grinned. "Hey, guess what! Sea turtles! I met one, and he was 150 years old!"

Several weeks later, Nemo was back home and ready for school. This time, so was Marlin. They raced to the bus stop, where an exchange student waited with the other kids. It was Squirt! "I'm from the EAC, dude!"

Three sharks passed by overhead. They parted to reveal Dory. "Thanks, guys!"

Her friend Bruce grinned back. "Well, we'll see you next week!" Dory swam beside Marlin, and Nemo waved goodbye. "Bye, Dad. Oh, wait! I forgot something!" He swam back and hugged Marlin. "Love you, Dad." Marlin smiled.

"I love you, too, son. Now, go have an adventure!"

The End